This book belongs to:

_____

MR BENN BIG TOP

MR BENN BIG TOP

DAVID McKEE

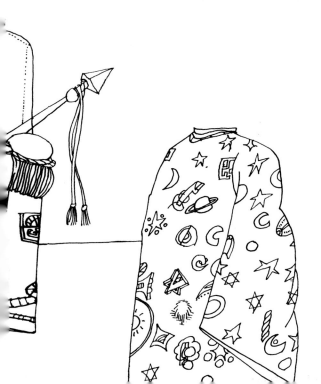

This edition first published in 2021 by Andersen Press Ltd.,
20 Vauxhall Bridge Road, London SW1V 2SA
First published as *Big Top Benn* by Dobson, London in 1980
Copyright © David McKee, 1980
The right of David McKee to be identified as the author and illustrator of this work
has been asserted by him in accordance with the Copyright, Designs and Patents Act, 1988.
All rights reserved. Printed and bound in China.
10 9 8 7 6 5 4 3 2 1
British Library Cataloguing in Publication Data available.
ISBN 978 1 83913 072 4

The sound of children laughing made Mr Benn look out of his window in Festive Road. He soon saw the cause of the laughter. Young Julian was wearing a mask and amusing his friends. "What a lovely sound," thought Mr Benn. "It must be fun to dress up and make people laugh." With that he remembered a costume shop that he knew, a special costume shop that adventures could start from. "There must be an outfit to make me look funny," he thought. He put on his hat and coat and set out for the shop.

As he walked, Mr Benn remembered adventures he'd had from the little shop. He reached the door and went in. When he saw the costumes again he almost decided to try something exciting instead of funny but before he did, as if by magic, the shopkeeper appeared.

"Good morning, sir," he said. "What would you like to try today?"

"Well," said Mr Benn, "I rather thought I'd like to make people laugh." The shopkeeper smiled and showed Mr Benn a baggy suit with a big bow tie.

"See if it fits, sir," said the shopkeeper and as Mr Benn took the suit towards the changing room he added, "This goes with it," and handed him a red false nose.

In the changing room Mr Benn put on the clothes. The suit was too big, the shoes were huge but when he put on the false nose and looked in the mirror he burst out laughing. "Perfect," he said and walked to the door, not the one to the shop but the one marked "TRYING ROOM". "I expect I'll come out into a circus," he thought.

He was wrong. He came out into open countryside. Nearby was a car, obviously intended for Mr Benn. It could only be a clown's car. Mr Benn jumped in and set off down the road.

At first it was just a pleasant country drive but as Mr Benn approached a bend in the road the car started to behave oddly. It bounced and banged and steamed and squeaked and wriggled and rattled and behaved like, well, like a clown's car. At the same time he came to a line of circus vehicles packed along the road. There was just room to pass.

At the front of the trucks stood the circus people with their backs to Mr Benn. As he approached they turned. He stopped the car, jumped out and tripped over. Everyone laughed. "Welcome," they said. "We can always use another clown."

"Could," said a voice. "Could use another clown if we could reach the next place for a show."

Then Mr Benn noticed that the road was blocked by boulders that had fallen in a storm. "They're too big to move," sighed the ringmaster, "and we can't turn the trucks in this narrow road."

"I can turn," said Mr Benn. "I'll see what help I can get," and he drove off back down the road.

Mr Benn had hardly left the circus when he saw a man walking over a nearby hill. "Perhaps he knows where I can get some help," thought Mr Benn and drove towards him. As he came closer Mr Benn could see that it was a very large man in a striped outfit.

Mr Benn recognised the man. It was Smasher Lagru, a convict he'd met on a previous adventure from the costume shop. "Smasher!" shouted Mr Benn in delight and held out his hand. Smasher stared, he didn't recognise Mr Benn in his clown's clothes. Mr Benn lifted off the nose. "123456789 Benn!" said Smasher. "This is a surprise." He explained that he'd been let out of prison and was off to find an honest job. Mr Benn laughed, he remembered that Smasher had got his name from smashing rocks in prison. "I've got a job for you," he said and told Smasher about the circus.

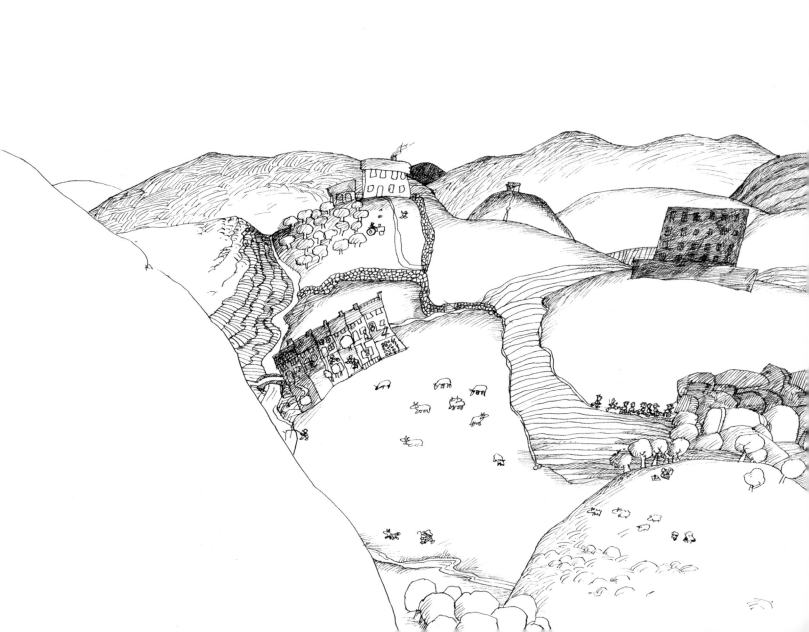

The circus people were disappointed to see Mr Benn return with just one man but when Smasher set to work with a sledgehammer they gasped. As Smasher smashed, the circus people cleared the small pieces of stone out of

the way. "If you want a job you could come with us," said the ringmaster. "You can be the strong man." Smasher was happy.

Once the way was clear the people started to cheer but the cheers turned to groans. The road should have passed over a bridge but the storm had destroyed that as well. They were faced with a huge gap.

"Don't worry," said Smasher "I'll fill the gap with boulders."

"That's no good," said Mr Benn. "You'd stop the river flowing."

Then everyone started to speak at once. The man who did tricks on stilts suggested making stilts for everybody. The tightrope walker wanted a rope across for them all to walk on. The balancing act wanted to balance pieces across the gap.

Mr Benn stopped them. "You are all thinking of ways that would get yourselves across," he said. "But that's not enough. Think of elephants on stilts, or trucks on tightropes. Even if we did manage to get everything across what about others who want to use this road? No, the circus works as a team and as a team we must build a bridge. Firstly we need wood to build with. Come on there are plenty of trees back along the road."

When enough trees were cut they started to build the bridge. "We'll make it on this side and slide it across," Mr Benn said.

The ringmaster was worried. "When we push the bridge across it will fall into the river," he said.

The balancing lady spoke up. "Make it longer than we need. The extra will stop it overbalancing. I'll watch it doesn't tip."

They started to make the bridge. As soon as they'd made a part they pushed a little over the edge. Then they built more on to it and pushed it a bit further. The more there was overhanging the more there was on the side. The piece of bridge on the road was always the longer.

"It would be useful to have some help on the other side to guide the bridge," said Mr Benn. The cowboy who did rope tricks lassoed a rock across the gap. The tightrope walker and trapeze artists soon crossed. The stilt man put on his longest stilts and stood in the river to help guide the bridge. They cut and carried, built and pushed, balanced and guided, lifted and pulled until eventually the bridge crossed the gap. Now they really did cheer.

The circus procession crossed the bridge and made their way to the
 next town.

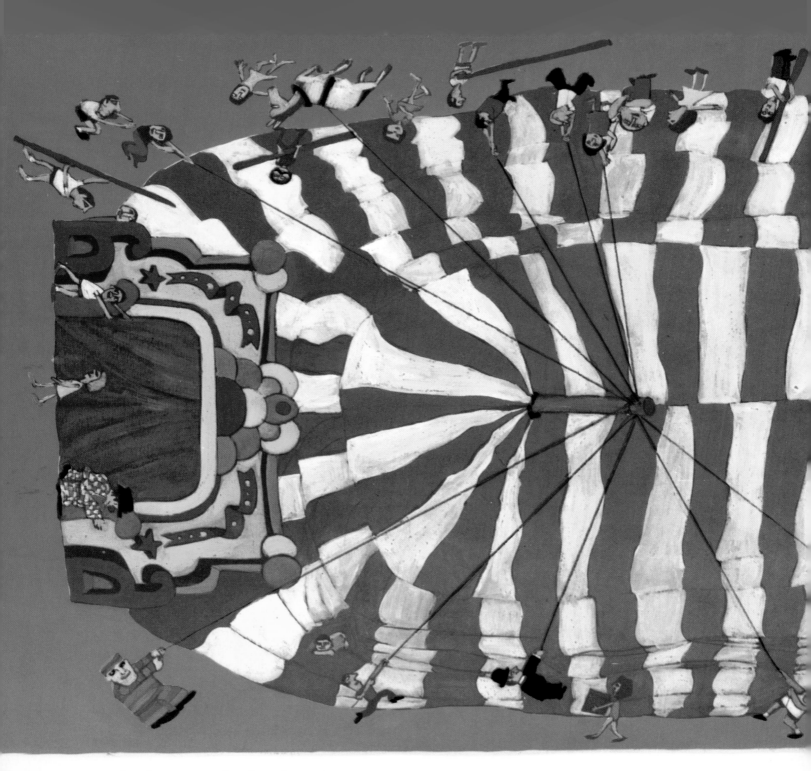

In the town the hard work started again as everyone set to to put up the big top, the circus tent.

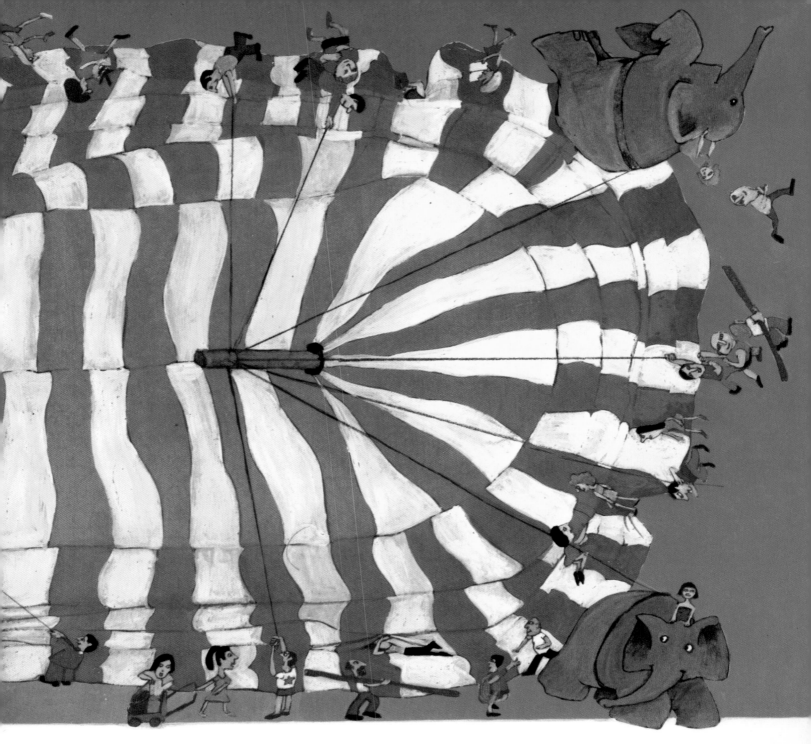

At last everything was ready for the show to begin.

The circus started with the parade of all the stars and animals.

After the parade the individual acts started. When it was Smasher's turn he was very popular. He was so strong. Mr Benn was glad that he'd found a job to suit him.

Then there was a magic act. Mr Benn thought he knew the magician but he couldn't remember seeing him at the bridge. He was very good. He made things change shape or move from one place to another or just suddenly appear.

Then the magician said, "I will now make a real live person vanish,
can I have a volunteer please?"
"Me, me," shouted Mr Benn and drove into the ring.
The car was doing its funny tricks.
It took ages for Mr Benn to reach the magician and how the crowd
laughed. "Step into this box please, sir," said the magician and
Mr Benn stepped into the brightly painted box.

Inside the box he was back in the changing room. He put on his own clothes and went into the shop. There stood the smiling shopkeeper. "Did you enjoy yourself, sir?" he asked.

"Yes thank you," said Mr Benn. "But there was a lot of hard work as well as laughs." Then he added, "You're a very good magician."

"We can all do something, sir," said the shopkeeper.

Mr Benn was just about to leave when he realised that he still had on the red nose. "You can keep that as a souvenir if you like, sir," said the shopkeeper.

"Thank you," said Mr Benn as he waved goodbye, "it will remind me not to wait too long before I come and see you again."

Collect the original Mr Benn books!

MR BENN'S BIG GAME — DAVID McKEE

MR BENN RED KNIGHT — DAVID McKEE

MR BENN 123456789 — DAVID McKEE